THANKS for the FEEDBACK

THINK...

Written by
Julia Cook

Illustrated by
Kelsey De Weerd

BOYS TOWN® Press

Boys Town, Nebraska

*To all of the seedlings out there
who need to be watered! ~ Julia*

Thanks for the Feedback... (I Think?)
Text and Illustrations Copyright © 2013, by Father Flanagan's Boys' Home
ISBN 978-1-934490-49-5

Published by the Boys Town Press
13603 Flanagan Blvd.
Boys Town, NE 68010

For a Boys Town Press catalog, call **1-800-282-6657**
or visit our website: **BoysTownPress.org**

Publisher's Cataloging-in-Publication Data

Cook, Julia, 1964-

Thanks for the feedback ... (I think?) : my story about accepting criticism and compliments ...
the right way! / written by Julia Cook ; illustrated by Kelsey De Weerd. -- Boys Town, NE :
Boys Town Press, c2013.

p. ; cm.
(Best me I can be ; 6th)

ISBN: 978-1-934490-49-5

Audience: grades K-6.
Summary: When a couple of friends give RJ a compliment, he just isn't sure how to respond.
When his teacher and parents tell him there are some things he needs to work on, his first re-
action is to argue and make excuses. RJ learns what it means to receive positive and negative
feedback, and how to respond appropriately, learning to accept and grow from criticism and
compliments at home, school and with friends.--Publisher.

1. Children--Life skills guides--Juvenile fiction. 2. Feedback (Psychology)--Juvenile fiction.
3. Interpersonal communication--Juvenile fiction. 4. Compliments--Juvenile fiction. 5. Praise-
-Juvenile fiction. 6. Criticism, Personal--Juvenile fiction. 7. [Interpersonal communication--
Fiction. 8. Compliments--Fiction. 9. Praise--Fiction. 10. Criticism--Fiction.] I. De Weerd,
Kelsey. II. Series: Best me I can be (Boys Town)

PZ7.C76984 T53 2013

E   1308

Printed in the United States
10 9 8 7 6

Boys Town Press is the publishing division of Boys Town,
a national organization serving children and families.

My name is RJ,
and sometimes when people
say things to me, I have a hard time
knowing what to say back.

3

One day after school,
Frankie and I were having a bubble gum
bubble blowing contest.
I blew a bubble that was about
29 times bigger than Frankie's.

He looked at me and said,
"You could go to the Olympics in bubble
blowing, and you'd win GOLD!"

4

When Frankie's words went into my head,
I started to think about what he had said.
I had no idea what to say back to him.
And then all my words just started to SWIM.

"No... I'm really not that good.
You're a lot better than I am," I said.

A few days ago, Norma the Booger Picker said, "Hey, RJ... I like your new bubble gum t-shirt."

Norma actually said something nice to me! She never does that!

When Norma's words
went into my head,
I started to think about what she said.
I had no idea what to say back to her.
Then all of my words turned into a **blur**.

"You just like it because it's green," I said.
"The same color as your boogers!"
Norma blew on her bangs, rolled her eyes at me, and walked away.
Then she didn't talk to me for the rest of the day.
(Which isn't such a bad thing!)

Then, yesterday, when we were playing soccer at recess, Sam said,
"Hey, RJ, you need to kick the ball with more of the side of
your foot when you shoot instead of using your toes."

When Sam's words went into my head,
I started to think about what he said.
I had no idea what to say back to him.
Then all of my words just started to SWIM.

"What do you know about shooting?" I said.
"You're a goalie, not a forward!"

Sam gave me a weird look. Then he shook his head,
wrinkled his eyebrows, and walked away.

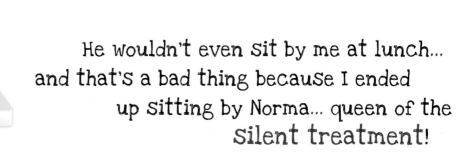

He wouldn't even sit by me at lunch...
and that's a bad thing because I ended
up sitting by Norma... queen of the
Silent treatment!

Last night, I had to go to parent-teacher conferences.
I have no idea why I had to go. I'm not a parent or a teacher!

"RJ," said my teacher, as we all took a seat,
"having you as my student is such a great treat!"

"Who? Me?"

"You're doing such a great job when it comes to spelling,
 and I'm very impressed with your storytelling!"

"You are?"

"You're also keeping your desk a whole lot *neater*,

and at our school play, you were an *excellent greeter*!"

"I was?"

"RJ, when it comes to your math, I just can't say enough! You're one of my best. You know all the *right stuff*!"

"I do?"

"We do need to talk about a few things.
    Sometimes your voice isn't as soft as it seems!"

"I know it's hard for you
    to stay in your seat,
But work time's the wrong time
    to try out your feet!"

"I feel that you still waste way too much time.
    Let's work on your focus, so that you *can shine*."

When my teacher's words went into my head,
I started to think about what she said.
I had no idea what to say back to her.
Then all of my words just turned into a **blur**.

14

"But I'm not the only one who talks out in class!"
   "I stay in my seat more than I used to!"
"And, I do focus... you just don't notice!"

   Just then, my mom reached over and tapped me on the knee under
      the table. That's her signal for, "RJ, STOP TALKING!" So I did.

When we got home that night, my parents made me sit at the kitchen table with them so we could talk about my conference.

"RJ," my mom said, "your teacher gave you
some really nice compliments tonight.
Why didn't you just tell her thank you?"

"When my teacher's words went into my head,
I started to think about what she said.
I had no idea what to say back to her.
Then all of my words just turned into a **blur**."

"RJ...

When somebody **GIVES** you a compliment,
The **BEST** thing for you to do,
Is to **LOOK** at the person, use a nice, pleasant voice,
And simply say, 'THANK YOU!' "

"Knowing the power of a compliment and
learning how to accept praise can make you
better and more successful in life."

18

"Then, RJ," my dad said, "your teacher gave you some great constructive feedback on how you can do better, and you kinda, sorta started to argue with her."

"But, Dad, when my teacher's words went into my head,
I started to think about what she said.
I had no idea what to say back to her.
Then all of my words just turned into a **blur**."

"RJ, feedback is a good thing.
   It's information that can help you improve
and grow. Most of the time when a person
      gives you feedback, it doesn't make you feel
good. But that's the price you have to pay
   for growing. The way you handle feedback
will make a difference in how other people
   treat you."

"Some people will give you mean feedback, and most of the time that's difficult to accept. You probably don't deserve mean feedback, but some people need to put others down so they can feel better about themselves. But just keep in mind, RJ, most feedback is just information."

Remember, RJ,
Feedback is
information

"When somebody GIVES you feedback,
They're helping to IMPROVE who you are.
LISTEN to the person, and say 'OK.'
Their words just might take you far.

Make sure that when you listen
You LOOK to the one who is talking to you.
STAY CALM on the inside, no matter what is said,
Then carefully THINK it through."

"Are there times in your class when you talk too loud or too much?"
　　"Yeah, I guess."

"Do you have a hard time staying in your seat during work time?"
　　"Yeah, I guess."

"Do you need to focus more in class so you don't waste your time?"
　　"Yeah, I guess."

"Well, RJ, I think your teacher was giving you great feedback."

About 39 years later, I got up from the kitchen table and went to bed. Before I went to sleep, I thought about everything my mom and dad told me. What they said really did make sense.

The next day at school, I used the sides of my feet
to kick the soccer ball just like Sam told me to,
and I made three goals during recess!

When the bell rang, Sam came up to me and
said, "You're AWESOME, RJ!"

I looked at him, smiled big, and said,
"Thanks!" just like my mom told me to.

MONDAY: Spelling Test

TUESDAY: Math Quiz

...rite a short story
...bout your hero

THURSDAY: Art / Computers

...ath Student
...ncement

During work time when my teacher gave me the **special signal** for sit down, stop talking, and start working, I picked up on it right away, really tried to focus, and I got all of my work done without wasting time!

At the end of the day, Bossy Bernice came over to my desk.

"You stink at math because you don't show all of the steps," she said.
"I bet you even copy off of other people so you can get the right answers."

When Bernice's words went into my head,
  I started to think about what she said.
  She called me a cheater, and that's kinda mean.
    But her information is not what it seems.

Maybe Bernice is just having a bad day.
    And, unfortunately, I happened to get in her way.
Maybe I should write down all of the steps.
    Then my teacher will know that I'm doing my best.

Bernice gave me feedback, and now I know
feedback is information that's helping me grow.

"I don't cheat, Bernice," I said. "But you're probably right.
I should write down all of my steps. Thanks for the tip!"

Teaching your child how to give and receive compliments is a very important life skill. Receiving sincere compliments successfully can help foster a child's self-worth and self-appreciation. Being able to give a sincere compliment to another person teaches a child how to recognize and appreciate others.

TIPS FOR GIVING AND ACCEPTING COMPLIMENTS

- Sincerity is the key to giving compliments.

- Praise is a good positive behavior reinforcement.

- Recognizing the power of compliments will help a child develop a more positive outlook on life and become more successful.

- Accepting compliments is a learned behavior and cannot be forced, so teach in the moment. Phrases that can help include:

  "This is when we say thank you."

  "Would you like to say thank you for that nice compliment?"

  "If you aren't comfortable with saying thank you, you can always smile and nod."

  Practice (role-play) playing the *"Thank You"* game.

If children can learn to consider and accept feedback that is given to them, they can use that feedback to improve.

TIPS FOR CHILDREN ON ACCEPTING FEEDBACK

- Keep in mind that feedback is simply information and/or advice that can help you improve. Most feedback is designed to help you!

- Don't take feedback personally. Most people are not trying to hurt you, they are just letting you know that their preferences may be different from yours.

- Being able to accept feedback shows maturity and can help prevent problems with people in authority.

- The way people handle feedback will determine how they are treated by others.

- Feedback doesn't always feel good, but being exposed to negative judgments is the price a person must pay for "growing."

- If feedback is difficult to accept, or if you don't agree with or understand what is said, talk to a trusted adult.

- There is no way to avoid getting feedback from others. We make big and small choices each day. With each choice comes the opportunity for someone to give you feedback.

- Keep in mind that some people give negative feedback to others so they can feel better about themselves. You may just be a person's target for the day. Learn to differentiate between sincere feedback that is meant to **help**, and mean feedback that is meant to **hurt**.

- Don't argue with feedback even if you don't agree. Trying to prove right and wrong will only increase anger and frustration on both sides. Just listen… who knows, that feedback may just make you better.

- Never let the fear of feedback stop you from doing what you want. Stay true to your own values and convictions.

- Listen without getting defensive and DON'T make excuses. Find out if you need to do something differently and then DO IT!

For more parenting information, visit boystown.org/parenting.

BOYS TOWN. Parenting

Boys Town Press Books
by Julia Cook

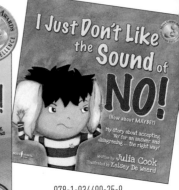

Kid-friendly titles to teach social skills

Reinforce the social skills RJ learns in each book by ordering its corresponding teacher's activity guide and skill posters.

978-1-934490-20-4
978-1-934490-21-1 (AUDIO BOOK)
978-1-934490-34-1 (SPANISH)
978-1-934490-23-5 (ACTIVITY GUIDE)

978-1-934490-25-9
978-1-934490-26-6 (AUDIO BOOK)
978-1-934490-53-2 (SPANISH)
978-1-934490-27-3 (ACTIVITY GUIDE)

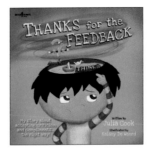

978-1-934490-28-0
978-1-934490-29-7 (AUDIO BOOK)
978-1-934490-32-7 (ACTIVITY GUIDE)

978-1-934490-35-8
978-1-934490-36-5 (AUDIO BOOK)
978-1-934490-37-2 (ACTIVITY GUIDE)

978-1-934490-43-3
978-1-934490-44-0 (AUDIO BOOK)
978-1-934490-45-7 (ACTIVITY GUIDE)

978-1-934490-49-5
978-1-934490-50-1 (AUDIO BOOK)
978-1-934490-51-8 (ACTIVITY GUIDE)

978-1-934490-67-9
978-1-934490-68-6 (AUDIO BOOK)
978-1-934490-69-3 (ACTIVITY GUIDE)

NEW TITLES

Building RELATIONSHIPS

A book series to help kids get along.

Making Friends Is an Art!
Cliques Just Don't Make Cents
Tease Monster
Peer Pressure Gauge
Hygiene...You Stink!
I Want to Be the Only Dog
The Judgmental Flower
Table Talk
Rumor Has It...

COMMUNICATE with Confidence

A book series to help kids master the art of communicating.

Well, I Can Top That!
Decibella
Gas Happens!
The Technology Tail

Responsible ME!

A book series to help kids take responsibility for their behaviors.

But It's Not My Fault
Baditude!
The Procrastinator
Cheaters Never Prosper
That Rule Doesn't Apply to Me!
What's in It for Me?

BoysTownPress.org

For information on Boys Town, its Education Model®, Common Sense Parenting®, and training programs:
boystowntraining.org | boystown.org/parenting
training@BoysTown.org | 1-800-545-5771

For parenting and educational books and other resources:
BoysTownPress.org
btpress@BoysTown.org | 1-800-282-6657